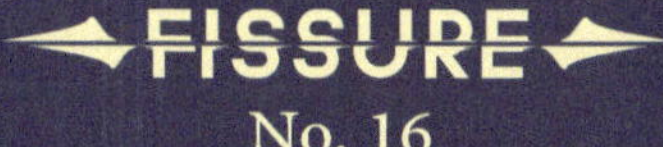

FISSURE
No. 16

ISBN: 978-1-956076-14-1

PROOFREADING and CREATIVE DIRECTION by NaBeela Washington
PROOFREADING by Keila Gallardo Cubas
LAYOUT and CREATIVE DIRECTION by Kristine Pham
COVER ART by Tran Nguyen and Emma Hodgdon

A Black journalist, poet, and art collector, NaBeela Washington holds a Master's in Creative Writing and English from Southern New Hampshire University and a Bachelor's in Visual Advertising from the University of Alabama at Birmingham. She is the Founder of Lucky Jefferson.

Keila Gallardo (she/he/they) is a freelance editor, translator and sometimes writer. He was born in Peru but is based in Canada. She hopes to keep being an editor who can bring variety to the industry. They enjoy writing, watching shows, listening to music and thinking too much about stories they like.

Tran Nguyen is a freelance graphic designer and aspiring environment concept artist from Vietnam. Inspired by illustrated stories and vivid imagination, Tran creates atmospheric designs that blend fantasy and realism. Her bold use of color brings immersive worlds to life. View her portfolio at tranarts. myportfolio.com.

Emma Hodgdon is an illustrator with experience in character design, comics, and children's book art. She's mentored young artists, assisted in classroom instruction, and studied at Maine College of Art and MassArt. Explore her portfolio at emmahodgdon.com.

Publication of Lucky Jefferson is made possible through community support.

Donate or submit to Lucky Jefferson at: luckyjefferson.com.

I begin this foreword from the suburbs of Chicago.

There is a thick silence permeating the air and I feel nauseous at the thought of being able to breathe *freely* right now. There is no rubble; no smell of decaying flesh; no ash to coffin the soul; no sounds of missiles piercing our sleep, setting homes ablaze. And these daily reminders break my heart.

I cannot fathom the perpetual fear that has kept Palestinian people up at night; the fear in doctors and paramedics working relentlessly despite diminished aid; the fear among journalists and press speaking out on the atrocities unfolding right before their eyes; the fear that blooms in children who will never return to school, their families, leaving this world too soon.

I am saddened at the increased censorship and doxxing of writers and editors, who have boldly professed they will not stand by and watch oppression win, yet again. *How* can we allow history to repeat?

The Trail of Tears. The Holocaust. Rwanda. Anatolia. Darfur. Haiti. Tulsa. Palestine.

My heart goes out to the people of Gaza, to Israelis, and those of the Jewish faith who do not support the mass slaughter and obliteration of an entire people. My heart goes out to the voices who will never speak again, from Palestine, from Israel, from the Congo, from Sudan, from Ukraine, and from other places buried beneath the darkness of these ongoing events.

The work in this issue reflects the darkness of our time, but it also screams our desire to be free.

If you are a writer or artist experiencing displacement, we invite you to lend your voice to our work. You will always have a voice with us, and we will forever stand with those who continue to be forcibly silenced.

We will never stop creating spaces where we can all be free.

NABEELA WASHINGTON
EDITOR-IN-CHIEF

MY DOCTOR TELLS ME THAT SHE CAN PRESCRIBE LEXAPRO IF I FIND THAT ANXIETY IS IMPACTING MY QUALITY OF LIFE

by Rachel Pittman

I'm not even anxious, it's just that there was hardly any snow this year. The sky over New York City burned ochre in June. Ten species of birds went extinct, honeycreepers native to Hawaii, Bachman's Warbler. A headline in *The Guardian*: "Grief is a Rational Response." There is a lag between extinction and its confirmation. A yellow songbird last sighted in 1988 is declared extinct forty years after the endling sang into a feathered void. If I think about the word 'endling' for longer than four seconds, I will start to cry. I'm not anxious, I'm just so rational that I want to scoop my brain out of my skull, rinse it off in cool water, wrap it in a soft white towel. Smother it. They say the earth's supply of freshwater will be sipped deep into the ground. Drought and famine. Tropical storms twirl like ballerinas on the Atlantic stage. They look beautiful on my phone screen—green, orange, red— while they shred through coastal towns. I swear I'm not anxious, it's just that the fireflies and bees are vanishing. On a tour of the Louisiana prairie, the biologist asked us, *how many butterflies have you seen this year*? And I realized, none. That was last April. The Age of Pollinators is ending, has ended already. How long until our air chokes us with soot? They're finding microplastics in breastmilk and placentas. I'm not anxious, I'm dreading the eventual collapse of infrastructure and institutions. Fascism is on the rise and our brains are swimming in bad news internet soup. Speaking of bad news, the side effects. *Nausea*, I can handle. It comes with the daily dread of living. *Insomnia*, I'm no stranger. *Headaches*, I'll fold myself into bed, turn off every light and imagine my brain a snail. *Fatigue*? Yes. *Excessive sweating*—summers are only going to get hotter from here. The sun licking our skin through a film of plastic. *Dry mouth*, I think it's wise to grow familiar with thirst. *Low libido*, oh well. Lexapro, I'll miss orgasms, but what a small price to pay to help me feel like the absence of birds.

DYSMORPHIA by Susan L. Lin

COMMUNAL EATING
by Angela Townsend

I am in favor of people eating, but I have not been people for some time. People eat when they are hungry and when they are not exactly hungry, and the roof remains intact either way.

People keep after-dinner mints in the butter compartment of their refrigerators and eat six in rapid succession. People order a second hash brown because the first was excellent. People handwrite lists three weeks before the holiday so they will remember the ingredients for feeding people.

People metabolize diagnoses and keep cooking. People make treaties with moderation and feast in peacetime. People have Type 1 and Type 2 and audition low-glycemic ginger snaps. People ask if I can eat that, and I don't know how to throw the question out of court. People know people whose dice rolled the same numbers as mine, and those people eat peanut butter kisses and pineapples sculpted like sunflowers, so why can't I?

People steeple their hands when I say food is my Gothic romance. People do not know what to do when I fidget with crusts and overcook metaphors. People keep asking if I can eat that, but they start giving candles instead of diabetic-safe gummy bears for Christmas. People hesitate to eat puddings around me until I reassure them I am glad people eat puddings. People ask me to pray for their people because I went to God college. People ask me to give the blessing even though I don't sit at the head of the table.

People close their mouths when I jump the buffet turnstile. People are excited about corn transfigured by cream. People are too excited about their plates to be ashamed that my salad is naked. People have sometimes deposited one raviolo on the corner of my plate where it does not touch the leaves. People always repatriate it without further debate. People are relieved when I put olives on my index fingers and pretend to conduct a symphony. People laugh at the noise cranberry sauce makes when it shimmies out the can, like a sausage in a gown two sizes too small.

People ask if I can just cover everything with insulin, like the other Type 1 they know. People know Type 1s who have mastered the high jump and eaten pretzels the size of a human face. People have watched Type 1s unfurl the cinnamon bun all the way to the nub. People were not there when the doctor taught me about "free foods" and my retinas. People who survive to adulthood all have to smile with guile until their cheeks hurt sometimes, so other people will not be ashamed. People may not have to do it when I do it, while passing the pies, but they all have to do it.

People say it is about control and Hollywood. People want to understand, but I cannot help them with my mouth shut. People would listen if I told them about sitting on the linoleum with a juice box in the dark, praying for spirit to reanimate body. People keep their hands busy when I say it wasn't a choice, but once I was not people anymore, I had to decide how I would pass the pies. People arrange marshmallows fat as cherubs on the sweet potatoes and bake them until they are singed but not burned.

People receive Communion without considering the calories. People step on the backs of each other's shoes and apologize with their eyes. People in the middle of the line remember what they forgot to confess, but it is too late to turn back. People are all pretty sure they have not been people for some time. People protest that naked salads are not a sin, not like the second slice or the soft belly. People are praying while I receive bread and wine.

BE HERE TO MOTHER ME AT THE END OF THE WORLD
by Disha Trivedi

In the mirror the skin under my eyes puckers like my mother's. I stretch it and think of women in stirrups. Of myself in stirrups. Crushing nurse fingers in my grip. Brown hand gone white as a sheet thrown over a child for Halloween. Medications needed to keep ghosts at bay get pulled off the tongue when a woman is pregnant to make her womb safe for the fetus. A fetus unborn is a ghost. My grandmother sings of her ghosts. Sang. Her illness rewrote the glass of her house with its books flush with English, a language not hers by birth. When she was younger, and alive, she handed down her first Shakespeare to my child hands. Pages moth-eaten, lacy like her skin as time tore her with its kisses. Weather-green, that book, the cover, like chutney, or the slick mint sari for a wedding I won't have. A shroud for the girl that I am with my under-eyes puckered into lips to kiss nothing. Once upon a time I ate Hamlet like a boy band, licked his cobwebs like cum. Now I am all flowers: rue and thyme and eyelashes like ripples of petals in water. Head filled with visions made between waking and pissing the pink that pulled me from sleep. Vomit enough and flowers will bloom around eyes, crushed vessels as purple as lavender sprigs. I woke wet at my legs like teenager flush from orgasm, or child left in sheets made nightmare-damp. Vomit in the toilet like a wet blond comma atop blood. Period returned after months disappeared. Gone rotten and brown on the panties curled into fist-shape, perfect for my lover to force into my mouth. Lace, lace, o lace! My reflection becomes an exam room. Some mornings I swear that I see my grandmother's ghosts in the mirror. But it's her ghost I look for. Her lacy fingers on pages thin as my eyelids. Doom'd for certain times to walk the night. List, list, o list! Mother of my mother, stay here for the hour, hands atop my spine's top, as battlement to walk, or mirror. Hold my hand while I'm in stirrups, birthing a mother for the future, bleeding a ghost out.

CHICAGO POEM
After Danez Smith

By Christiana Castillo

Juj tells me to *write the Chicago poem* after talking about how our sadness makes sense here, despite being away from you and your oceans, all the places where our ancestors knew vastness. We get to know the waters of Lake Michigan instead. Our own vastness holds us. Chicago winters remind us to take Vitamin D again and again. We attempt to swallow sunlight. I learn to trust capsules of medicine, the way Lake Michigan looks when the sun brushes her waters after freezing temperatures. How the sunrays create steam that spreads the golden blue sunrise across LSD like a watercolor painting. We know the feeling of soil thawing under our feet, the way crocuses and daffodils rise, just like that. The gift of intermittent spring's arrival. We've memorized the progression to summer, how things go grey to green like no time has passed. It's seamless, like hummingbirds pulling nectar. The monarch butterfies return, the hummingbirds return, the people return in ways I'm still trying to understand.

México, do you know the feeling of seasonal depression being snatched out of your body? It goes slowly, and then all at once, like hummingbird eggs hatching. I've tracked my moods, I know what it is to feel like I am part of the disembodied sea of people waiting for sunlight, waiting for the deliverance of *summertime Chi*. México, have you ever been part of something like that?

And México, my skin was never supposed to be this pale, but god there's something about what it's like to have winter stacked against you. The sky an endless gray, and you still might be the brightest thing around. México, it makes you want to outlive what's frozen. Have you ever felt like that?

México, when was the last time you tried to duplicate the sun? Why is it that my sister tells me to wait until summer to feel like myself again? México, do you always feel like yourself? Have you ever yearned for laughter radiating off of concrete? México, when was the last time you felt something temporary?

México, have you ever seen everything around you die or get up and leave? The grass gone yellow, the trees barren, no flowers outside to admire, the hummingbirds all gone, the monarchs turn to you instead of Chicago. I've seen my corner of the world die and come back to life countless times. Do you know what I mean?

BLOOD QUANTUM MATH

By Jessi Farfan

Name: _______________________

Tribe: _______________________

Roll #: _______________________

1. If Sarah's grandmother was half Choctaw and married a white man, and their daughter married another white man, what fraction of Sarah's granddaughter is legally Indian?

a) 1/2

b) 1/4

c) 1/8

d) The Bureau of Indian Affairs says she does not qualify.

---

2. Jeremy's family has lived on the same reservation land for 4 generations. His cousin has lived in the city for 26 years. How much better of an Indian is Jeremy than his cousin?

a) 100%

b) 76.17%

c) 0%

d) 19.68%

---

3. Maria has a Certificate of Degree of Indian Blood that says 1/32. People say she looks like her white mom, not her indigenous dad. She attends powwows, makes her own regalia, is an intermediate speaker of her ancestral language, and prays every morning. Her cousin is visibly native but was "raised white." Who is more indigenous?

a) The one with the looks

b) The one with the prayers

c) They are equally native

d) Ask the nahullo who wrote the test

---

4. Below is a graph representing the percentage of Choctaw people living on ancestral lands.

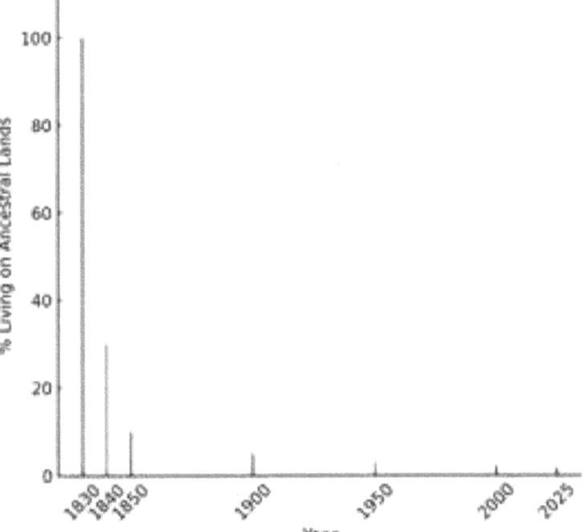

If the population began at 100% in 1800 and declined steadily until they reach statistical invisibility, what year did Indians go extinct?

a) 1831, when the government called it policy

b) 1924, when they granted citizenship

c) 2020, when the census left them out

d) 2025, when the murder rate for our women was 10 times more than the national average.

5. Convert your existence into an acceptable format. Show your work.

---

6. Your father drank himself into a stupor every day. He never taught you the language, but taught you how to flinch. He said he was "raising you tough." Didn't say for what. All the other adults in your life normalized his behavior. What percentage of Native Americans are alcoholics?

a) 45.2%
b) 50%
c) 13.6%
d) 0%, we just like to party

---

7. A white anthropologist calls your people "culturally extinct." Meanwhile, your grandma is still in her kitchen cooking walakshi. Years later, a museum quietly repatriates 206 of your ancestors' bones under a law meant to return the dead to tribes they once claimed didn't exist. If five white voices declare you gone, and one Native voice says otherwise, when do they ignore it?

a) Immediately
b) After peer review
c) When the grant money runs out
d) Before you even open your mouth

8. You post about indigenous issues on social media. Someone replies: "That was centuries ago." Then they repost an AI "never forget 9/11" graphic. If history cannot make colonization look bad, what history books are read?

a) The ones with Columbus on the cover
b) The ones that call genocide "relocation"
c) The ones that skip the part where we fought back
d) The ones that start after our removal

---

9. Refer to the diagram below.

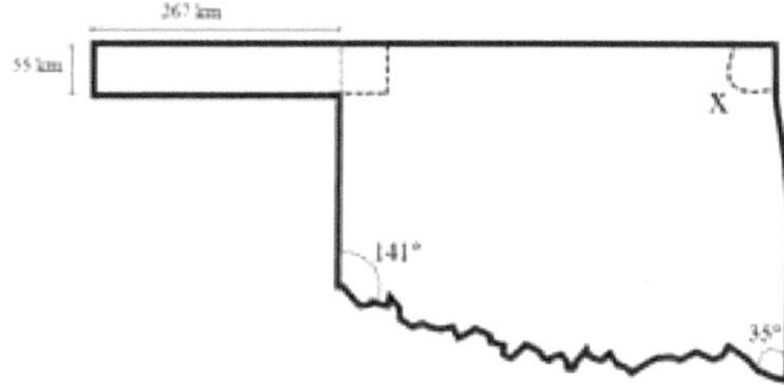

Let X represent the percentage of Native Americans who disappeared due to colonization. Let the rest represent farmland, oil leases, subdivisions, and stories about how "my great-great-grandmother was a Cherokee princess." Solve for X.

WORKER'S SELF-ASSESSMENT

By A.J. Frantz

Never / rarely / sometimes / often / very often

How often do you have   difficulty
      paying attention
when you are doing boring or repetitive work?

                Repeatedly

never
often   restless / scattered
            fidgety

How   sometimes
      do you often feel
distracted by activity   around you?

Do you very / sometimes
feel high-octane
often overly active, compelled
to do things as if driven
by a motor?

Rarely / sometimes / never

chug on, brittle pistons
firing through plosive iron

Work on, eyes up   attentive
                in activity,
     fueled and pulled
          ahead by each cog   tick
tick tick / very often
push forward
always.

Greetings from

FREAK OUT

CANYON

FUCK

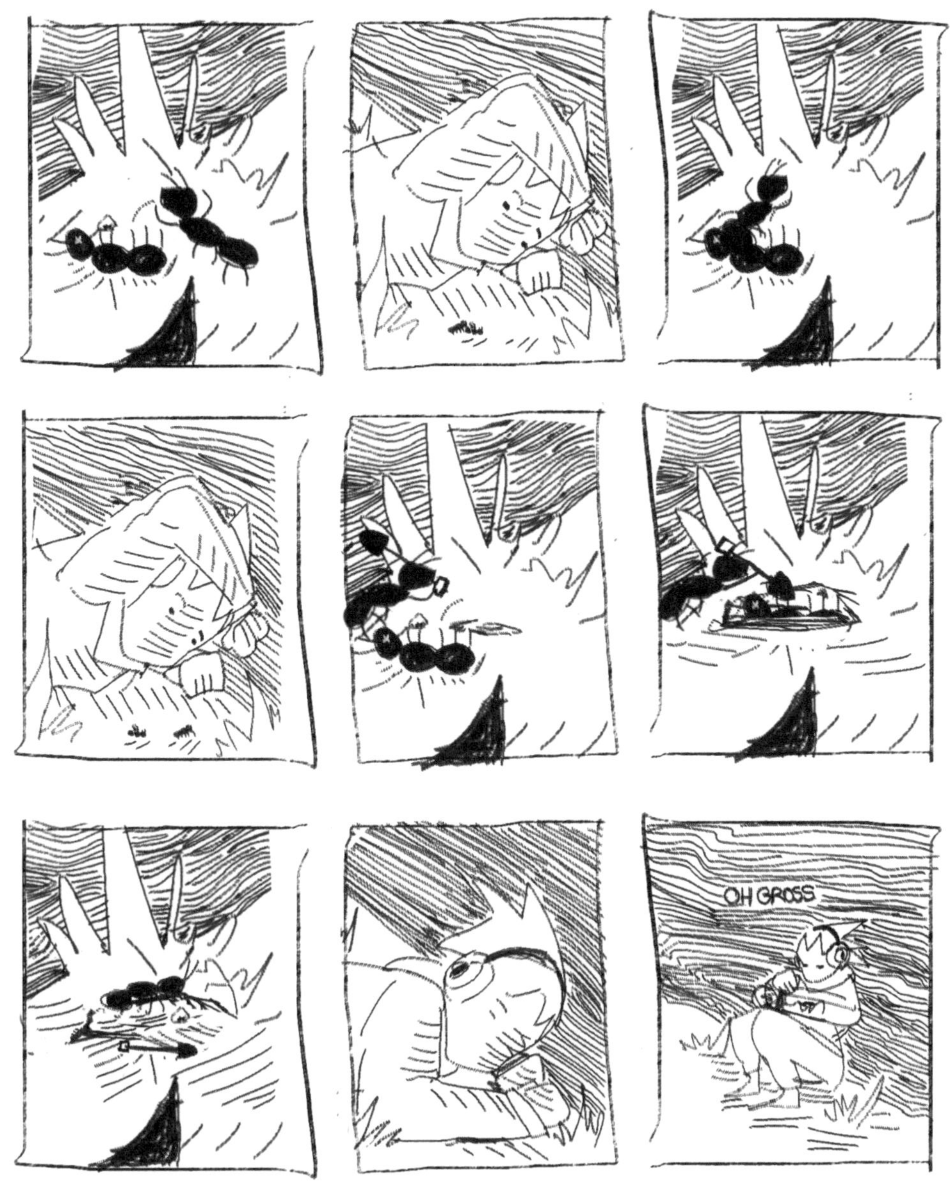
OH GROSS

MODERN INNER DIALOGUE

By K.R. Van Horn

Cultural shrinkflation, tariffs, and Adderall. Social media receipts. Organic avocados. Terms and conditions. Normalization of psychic, social, and student debt. Entitlement in racist, late-stage surveillance capitalism. Rent hikes and monetization of commodified digital avatars and identities embedded in fake news feeds. Blue light flickers. Tickers filled with fires, riots, Gaza. Diddy memes. Foodies. AI drone conspiracy theories. Big Pharma. Privileged Russian bots trolling Bluetooth Zoom meetings. Whataboutism living rent-free in my trauma-triggered vaccinated, podcast, Paxil-Prozac-packed head. Quantum physics aliens. Rogan. Ozempic ads, caffeinated main character energy, algorithms shadowbanning and de-platforming all mis-, dis-, and mal-information. Gaslighting, gatekeeping, toxic positivity and masculinity. Lebron-Bernie boundaries of doom-scrolling. Set screen time. Dig deep into Deep States. Deepfakes. Defund donut police states. Pivot on political hot takes. Curse climate change HEVs and neoliberal Trumpist New World Order consumer Marxism. Extreme identity bipartisan postmodern socialism. Black Lives Matter. Politically correct terrorists at the border sneer at radical populism and narcissistic, clout-chasing, performative, unsustainable, parasocial woke relationships with right-wing transgender influencers and fascist activist actors. Paid-for Putin-Pelosi apologists and politicians. Attention-slash-grift Austrian economic system built on the weaponization of trust, disillusionment, and marijuana paranoia. Fentanyl bias is calculated and used to control through propaganda and bad actors with hot-dog whistles. Musk virtue signaling illegal big tech space data immigration policy in cryogenic echo chambers. Marginalized BlackRock-Blackwater allies. Pseudo-academic critical race critics, anthropologists, and theorists. China. Life partners unpack with medicated talking heads. Quit quietly. Disengage from narratives. Binge-watch streaming reality game shows. Consume Viagara, Xanax, and Highballs. Build your brand. Take ten thousand steps. Eat the rainbow. Stay present. Seek self-care. Seek solace. Seek. Seek spirituality, balance in the reality of neurodivergent COVID cognitive dissonance, killing beach vibes in real-time. It all has me metaverse gaming. Masking up. Asking: What happens when the scaffolding finally collapses?

AFTER THE ELECTION, PEOPLE ASK HOW I AM

By Lynne Schilling

My mind takes refuge in the Merritt Parkway tunnel near the New Haven-Woodbridge exit. It presses itself against the wall. Fears drive past at dizzying speeds. My neck and jaw spasm with pain, persistent and raw. Stomach lingers in the kitchen, searching for chocolate. My feverish heart stays in bed. Shades are pulled against reality; the television is mute. My heart cannot bear the burden of news. Hope lies crumpled at the bottom of the staircase, surrounded by EMTs who argue about where to place the brace.

Before the hyacinth
Glacial
Winter.

AFTER JOHN BOY

By Shaniqua Harris

After John Boy died on the steps of the church, while the choir had been practicing too passionately to hear his last breaths, his mother destroyed the church. She ripped the flowers from the altar and stamped them until they stained the tiles and would have made her fall if her rage wasn't keeping her steady. She ripped the wood from the altar, and from the stage uncovering the baptismal pool that was only used when the sea was unagreeable. She threw the pews, each of which had taken two grown men to carry into the church, clear across the room where they chipped and became unsteady.

She tore took the hymnbooks and the tambourines and the spare cymbals for the drum and the drum sticks and all the spare electrical equipment, including cables she did not know the use of, and she splintered the wood in her hands and twisted the metal until not even someone with time and patience could hammer out the dents and make the instruments usable again.

The shutters quivered with her screams, and she tore them from their windows. Tossing them onto the pews. Then tossing them where the altar had been. Then throwing the pews after them, breaking whatever legs had dared to not break. She did not touch the bibles. Even in her rage she could not bring herself to touch them, though her own bible which she had been praying over in John Boy's absence, as she always did, was lying beside the path she'd carved as she ran to the church.

Pastor Blackman stood outside, the entire village behind him, and did not dare enter. He had been watching the choir practice, forming his sermon in their cadence. His own son, Nige, another good boy destined for anything he wanted, had been the one to find the body and start the alarm. Nige had been on his way home from the extra lessons he took twice a week. He always came to the church before going home, hoping to spend a few minutes alone with his father, before they went back home to his mother and siblings who were full of life and laughter and love and much too much for him.

Nige had found John Boy slumped over. His eyes closed the way he did when he prayed, and Nige had thought his friend was playing dead. He'd touched him, shaken him, tried to wake him and when he didn't, he called for his father. His father called for the choir to stop singing, and for Brother Alleyne, whose wife had been a nurse at the hospital, to call for his wife to come. The choir scattered, first checking on John Boy to see if it was true, then running up the road and down the road and through the gaps in the fences, calling for anyone who could help or who knew where his mother was.

Nige was still standing over the body, staring at his hands, when John Boy's mother arrived. He didn't flinch as she began to scream. He didn't flinch as the noise of her destruction filled the night. He didn't notice his father standing near him nor the crowd that begun to gather around him.

His own mother came and tried to hold him, and he looked at her as if he had never seen her before. She tried to pull him away, and his feet would not move. He finally looked at his father and they looked at each other and did not say anything.

Pastor Blackman's mind was full of verses he usually quoted to the bereaved, the verses he recited at funerals, the verses he placed in the hands and mouths of grieving mothers. He listened to the destruction, looking at his son and thinking of verses that filled his mouth with bitterness, looking at the dead boy who had grown alongside his own son and who was also like a son to him.

John Boy's mother left the church and the earth reverberated under her feet as she walked to the sea. The place second to God in the village. The sea had baptised them, christened them, washed the vermix off their skin. The sea gave them fish to eat, water to desalinate when the water was cut off and there was no rain. The sea bathed them and held them soft but also punished them. The crowd followed her, holding hands and arms, and John Boy's body high above them wrapped in a tablecloth someone had ripped off a clothesline.

John Boy's mother careened through the sand until she found his father's boat. She kicked the boat and peeled long strips of paint from it with her nails until its name *Dream* lay on the sand. Then she kicked the sand over it, burying it in a shallow mound. She pushed the boat, rocking it in the rhythm of her wails.

His father had been selling his day's catch, his pockets awaiting the money that he would soon spend on a bottle of rum, half a grilled chicken, and whatever else the rumshop woman had cooked to sell. He'd come running when the news reached him, the money still in his hands, wet with sweat and crumpled in anger. He stood with the crowd, and his anger rippled until the crowd was riled. He stood now, behind her, cradling his son for the first time.

He went to the other side of the boat, lay his son in it, and unwrapped his body from the tablecloth and laid it over him like a blanket. He remembered the many times his son had gone fishing with him and been terrified of the water, the fish, the heat of the sun, getting trapped in the nets or jukked by a hook, and had begged to go home. How he had taken him home to his mother each time, and how his son would again, days later, begin to beg to go fishing again.

John Boy's parents stood on either side of the boat and looked at him as they pushed the boat to the tide. The sea lapped their ankles, and they kept looking at him, their son, or rather his body. Each remembering him as the unanticipated proof of a love seventeen summers past. Each wishing that they had made him stay home that night or kept him locked away at home his whole life or sent him away to a better place where he could be both happy and safe.

They looked at him, and did not look at each other, with regret.

Pastor Blackman stood by the boat, looking at this boy who had played with his son, been baptised with his son, taken communion with his son, been a brother to his son. When he'd baptised John Boy, he had been afraid of the water and had trembled, clinging onto the hands and robes around him, gasping for breath as he'd risen from the water. He cupped sea water in his hands and let it fall over John Boy's face. He wiped a thumb over the face, washing away dirt, blood, and sand. He used his handkerchief to dry the face.

Other men who preached in the church came and cupped sea water over the body, letting it wash away the blood, fluids, and other signs of death. They did not pray. Not even Brother James who was the oldest man in the village and had seen many deaths.

The crowd came one at a time to look at John Boy, to touch him, to adjust the tablecloth, and softly call his name, to dip out the defiled sea water with their hands. They paused over him, trying to reconcile the memories they had of a boy who always smiled, helped, and never complained. The boy they trusted their daughters with and hoped their sons would emulate. The boy whose voice was quiet when he spoke but sang in a baritone that moved them when they persuaded him to sing solo. The boy who was smart and who they knew would leave one day, but not like this. They knew he would go to university, somewhere far, far away where he would learn to be a Doctor or a Lawyer or an Engineer. The boy they knew would leave, and maybe come back one day, but who would take them, their pride, with him.

Nige came to the boat last and pulled himself into it and sat by the head.

John Boy's father and his mother looked at him and understood that he would go with them. They pushed the boat further out until it rode the water and then they pulled themselves into it.

The sea carried the boat until the moonlight bathed it.

MOURNING JOE

By Kashawn Taylor

Last Friday,
around half past ten
in the ghastly winter gloom
of an overcast New England morn,
two old men came to my job,
ordered lunch, took advantage
of our free senior coffee

    a pump or two
    of vanilla, creamer in a cup
    on the side

How they moved
with such precise calculation
as though one wrong maneuver
would tear the delicate fabric
of their two-man universe apart
How they laughed,
their bodies thick with wool jackets, hats;
the lines on their faces,
deep & permanent, as if carved
by time with deadly intention,
writhed with every Good one, Joe!

& how I watched, I stared
with deadly intention as Joe fell
asleep while other Joe took a leak
& like a fist to the chest,
it hit me:

I am 32, which is close
to 35, which we all know
is actually 40 & what
have I done with my Time?
& who will sit across
from me when even respiration
requires concentration sipping
burnt fast food coffee?
& what will I leave behind
for my nieces and nephews
whom I long to know like family,

for this world,
which may never truly accept me,
only see me as a felon
because our past selves may die
but never fully decompose?

Morning, Joe!
Would you like a refill of your coffee?

STORM

By Nicholas Pagano

Even that part, too, the love
being struck by it, gives way
to a need for shelter—

but I can never say when
enough is enough, or why
to decide looks like nothing

but pattern. An oak
shivered by rain and wind,
trying to prove its truth

sturdiest. Silver nail, little
silver that pins wings for now
to the branches deepest.

Between the leaves. Look
how all this can be
measured against these clouds.

Cascade falls, in search of winter
by Alexandra Nwigwe

Spot illustrations by
Riley Hannon (pages 7, 8, 24, 28, 33) and
Thy Hoang (pages 15, 23)

➤ MEET THE CONTRIBUTERS ➤

9   Rachel Pittman is a PhD student at Georgia State University where she teaches writing and serves as an Assistant Editor at Five Points. Her writing has appeared or is forthcoming in miniskirt magazine, Whale Road Review, Strange Horizons, and Fairy Tale Review.

10   Susan L. Lin is a Taiwanese American storyteller who hails from southeast Texas and loves to dance. Her novella GOODBYE TO THE OCEAN won the 2022 Etchings Press novella prize, and her literary/visual art has appeared in nearly a hundred publications. Find more at https://susanllin.com.

11-12   Angela Townsend is a five-time Pushcart Prize nominee and seven-time Best of the Net nominee. Her work appears or is forthcoming in Arts & Letters, Chautauqua, Pleiades, SmokeLong, and West Trade Review, among others. She graduated from Princeton Seminary and Vassar College and works for a cat sanctuary.

13   Disha Trivedi is from Northern California. Her poetry and fiction appear in Rust & Moth, Rogue Agent, The Harvard Advocate: The Women's Issue, and elsewhere. She lives in New York City.

14-15   Christiana Castillo (she/ella) is a Mexican-Brasilian-American poet,educator, cultural worker, and gardener born in Rio de Janeiro, Brasil, raised in Southeastern Michigan, and currently based out of Nashville, TN. Previous work of hers can be found in Room Magazine, The Pinch Journal, Belt Magazine, The Acentos Review, The Detroit Metro Times, The Chicago Reader, among others. Her poetry chapbook, Crushed Marigold, was published in 2020 with Flower Press.

16-17   Jessi Farfan is a Choctaw writer who thinks blood quantum should be illegal and sarcasm should count as medicine. Their work is kind of like a heckler at a land acknowledgement. She loves to write poems that make your fingers sweat and smudge those fake colonial borders. Their work can be found in MORIA.

18   A. J. Frantz is from Detroit and currently studies urban planning at Oberlin College. Her work has appeared in Folio, Meniscus, Prime Number Magazine, ellipsis, and elsewhere.

19-21   Josie Levin is a Chicago based artist and writer whose comic work has appeared in the Florida Review and carte blanche. You can see more of Josie's art and writing on his instagram @ bemusual. Josie is currently a Poet-In-Residence at the Chicago Poetry Center.

22   K.R. Van Horn is writing full-time from an oceanfront patio in the tropics. That's not true. He has kids to raise and bills to pay, so he lives in South Korea with his family, things, and ideas. But the writing never stops. Follow him at @krvanhorn.bsky.social & @krvanhorn (X)

23   Lynne Schilling got serious about writing poetry at age 75. Her poems have appeared in Adelaide Literary Magazine, Quartet, Humana Obscura, and The Alchemy Spoon. She has poems forthcoming in Braided Way Magazine. One of her poems recently won Honorable Mention in the 2024 Barbara Mandigo Kelly Peace Poetry Contest.

24-28   Shaniqua Harris is a Barbadian Brit based in London. She has a BA and an MA in Creative Writing and is pursuing a PhD. She primarily writes about women, the world, her life, and the Caribbeanness of it all. Previously published in Fruitslice and MIR Online.

29   Kashawn Taylor is a Black, queer, formerly incarcerated writer from Connecticut.

30   Nicholas Pagano has previously been published in Mid-Atlantic Review, Stone Circle Review, Chronogram, Field Guide, and elsewhere. He lives and writes in New York.

30-31   Alexandra Nwigwe is a designer, engineer, and writer from New Jersey where she finds solace in making art with her hands and capturing her memories, whether through poetry or photography.

◄SUBMIT TO LUCKY JEFFERSON►

Lucky Jefferson's mission is simple: we publish social change.
And our vision is to see books reimagined to center the modern reader.

Founded in 2018, Lucky Jefferson is an award-winning non-profit, journal, and publisher that reimagines books by creating interactive and collaborative community experiences that center the writer and artist and cultivate inclusion and representation in contemporary literature.

Lucky Jefferson is proud to feature poets and writers who have never been published, marginalized perspectives, and those who sought to pursue writing later in life.

Learn more + consider submitting at: luckyjefferson.com

www.ingramcontent.com/pod-product-compliance
Lightning Source LLC
Chambersburg PA
CBHW041925180726
48295CB00003B/83